This book belongs to

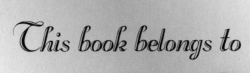

Lily Lily Lily
Lily

Disney fairies

TinkerBell

A READ-ALOUD STORYBOOK

Adapted by
Lisa Marsoli

Illustrated by
Jeff Clark, Adrienne Brown, Charles Pickens,
and the Disney Storybook Artists

Random House New York

Copyright © 2008 Disney Enterprises, Inc. All rights reserved. Published in the United States by Random House Children's Books, a division of Random House, Inc., 1745 Broadway, New York, NY 10019, and in Canada by Random House of Canada Limited, Toronto, in conjunction with Disney Enterprises, Inc. Random House and colophon are registered trademarks of Random House, Inc. Library of Congress Control Number: 2008922050   ISBN: 978-0-7364-2529-2

www.randomhouse.com/kids/disney

Printed in the United States of America

10 9 8 7 6 5 4

On a chilly winter's night in London, a baby lay peacefully in her crib. As her mobile twirled, the baby let out her very first laugh and—as with all first laughs—a fairy was born!

The laugh floated out the window and attached itself to a dandelion wisp. It flew above the human world straight toward the Second Star to the Right, and through a burst of light into Never Land!

The laugh floated toward Pixie Hollow, a magical place in the heart of Never Land where the Never fairies lived.

"Oh, my! Come on! Let's go!" the fairies cried. They followed the laugh as it made its way toward the Pixie Dust Tree.

A dust-keeper named Terence sprinkled some pixie dust on the laugh. It made a tinkling sound and took the shape of a fairy.

Queen Clarion approached. "Born of laughter, clothed in cheer, happiness has brought you here. Welcome to Pixie Hollow," she said.

The newcomer flapped her wings. She could fly!

Queen Clarion waved her hand and some toadstools sprang up. Fairies began to place objects on them. Rosetta, a garden fairy, brought a flower. A water fairy named Silvermist carried a droplet of water. Iridessa, a light fairy, had a glowing flower lamp, while a fast-flying fairy named Vidia set down a whirlwind.

"These objects will help you find your talent," the queen explained.

The new fairy timidly placed her hand on the flower. Its glow instantly faded. She reached for the water droplet, but its glow faded, too. Then she touched the whirlwind—and it disappeared.

The new fairy was discouraged. But as she passed the hammer, it started to glow. Then it flew straight to her!

"I've never seen one glow that much," said Silvermist. Rosetta agreed. "Li'l daisy-top might be a very rare talent indeed!"

Vidia fumed. *She* had one of the strongest and rarest talents in Pixie Hollow, and she wasn't looking for competition.

"Come forward, tinker fairies," called the queen, "and welcome the newest member of your talent guild—Tinker Bell!"

"Haydee hi, haydee ho! I'm Clank!" boomed a large tinker fairy.

"We're pleased as a pile of perfectly polished pots that you're here," added Bobble, a tinker who wore dewdrop glasses.

"You have arrived at a most wondrous and glorious time!" Clank said as they flew above Pixie Hollow.

"It's almost time for the changing of the seasons!" added Bobble.

"Welcome to Tinkers' Nook!" Bobble announced
after a little while.

Tinker Bell saw a small courtyard lined with twig-
and-leaf cottages. Fairies were fixing and fashioning
all kinds of amazing, useful objects.

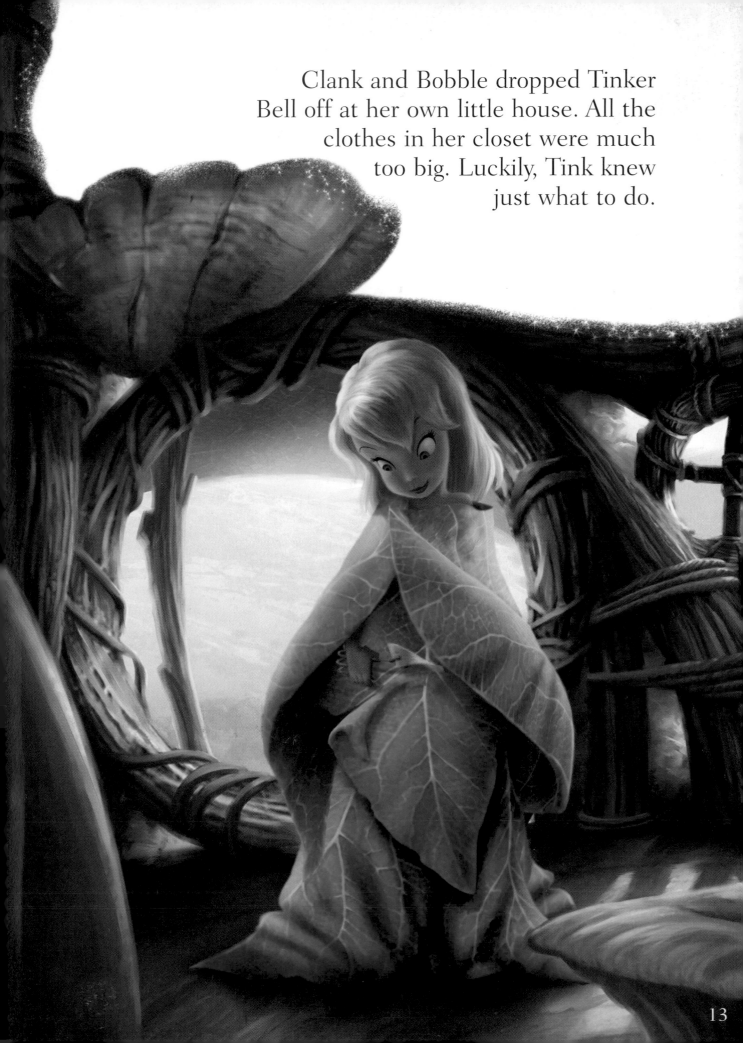

Clank and Bobble dropped Tinker Bell off at her own little house. All the clothes in her closet were much too big. Luckily, Tink knew just what to do.

Tinker Bell put on her new dress, tied her hair up, and reported to the workshop.

Soon Fairy Mary—the no-nonsense fairy who ran Tinkers' Nook—arrived.

"So dainty!" Fairy Mary exclaimed as she looked at Tink's hands. "Don't worry, dear, we'll build up those tinker muscles in no time."

Then, after reminding Clank and Bobble to make their deliveries, Fairy Mary was gone.

A little while later, Tink, Clank, and Bobble set out to deliver some springtime items to the nature fairies, with help from Cheese the mouse.

Suddenly, the fairies heard a sound behind them. *PITTER-PATTER! PITTER-PATTER!*

"Sprinting Thistles! *Aaaaagh!*" screamed Clank. The weeds nearby had come to life and were rushing toward them!

The wagon flew down the path and crashed in the middle of Springtime Square.

Thankfully, the tinkers were unhurt. They began to make their deliveries. There were milkweed-pod satchels for an animal fairy named Fawn, pussy willow brushes for Rosetta, and rainbow tubes for Iridessa.

Silvermist was there, too. She sprayed water into the air. When Iridessa flew through the droplets, a perfect rainbow was formed. Iridessa rolled it up into a tube.

"I'm going to take it to the mainland," she explained to Tink.

"What's the mainland?" the new fairy asked.

"It's where we're going for spring, to change the seasons," replied Silvermist.

Next, the tinkers stopped at the Flower Meadow. Vidia zipped by, using her whirlwind to pull pollen from the flowers.

"Hi!" said Tinker Bell. "What's your talent?"

"I am a fast-flying fairy," answered Vidia. "I make breezes in summer and blow down leaves in autumn. Fairies of every talent depend on me."

"Tinkers help fairies of every talent, too!" Tink said excitedly.

"*I* make forces of nature. *You* make pots and kettles," Vidia pointed out. "It's not like spring depends on you."

"When I go to the mainland, I'll prove just how important we are!" Tink replied.

"I, for one, am looking forward to that," Vidia said, rolling her eyes.

Tink flew off, grumbling to herself. Soon, however, she was distracted by something shiny down on the beach. She flew closer. It was a coin!

Tink began digging. Before long she had found all sorts of treasures. She scooped them up and took them to the workshop.

"Lost Things," said Clank when Tink arrived.

"They wash up on Never Land from time to time," said Bobble. "Not much good for anything, though."

Fairy Mary whisked Tink's trinkets away. The Queen's Review of the springtime preparations was that night, and there was still a lot to do.

Tink knew this was her chance to prove just how important a tinker's talent really was!

That evening, the Minister of Spring welcomed Queen Clarion to the review ceremony. "When the Everblossom blooms, we will be ready to bring spring to the mainland," he said proudly.

Suddenly, Tinker Bell arrived. "I came up with some fantastic things for tinkers to use when we go to the mainland!" she called.

Before the queen could say anything, Tink pulled out a homemade paint sprayer. But instead of spraying color, it exploded, making a huge mess!

The queen looked at Tinker Bell kindly. "Tinker fairies don't go to the mainland," she said. "All the springtime work is done by the nature fairies. I'm sorry."

Tink returned to the workshop. "Being a tinker stinks," she grumbled.

"Excuse me?" replied Fairy Mary.

"Why don't we get to go to the mainland?" Tink asked.

"The day you can magically make the flowers grow or capture the rays of the sun, you can go. Until then, your work is here," said Fairy Mary impatiently.

Suddenly, Tink smiled slyly. She had an idea.

The next morning, Tink found her friends at the Pixie Dust Well.

"If you could teach me your talents, maybe the queen would let me go to the mainland," Tink said.

No fairy had ever changed his or her talent! Reluctantly, Tink's friends agreed to help.

Silvermist was first. The water fairy showed Tink how to place a dewdrop on a spiderweb.

But each time Tink tried, the dewdrop burst.

Next, Iridessa demonstrated how to give fireflies their glow. She captured light in a bucket and scattered it. Dozens of fireflies flew through it and lit up.

But when Tink tried, the light wouldn't stick to her fingers. She threw the bucket in frustration. The light spilled in every direction. Now she was glowing, too!

The fireflies swarmed around her—they thought she was the most beautiful thing they had ever seen!

Fawn had Tink's animal-fairy lesson all planned. "We're teaching baby birds how to fly," she announced.

Fawn showed Tink what to do.

Unfortunately, Tink's bird was terrified. He didn't want to go anywhere.

Tink saw a majestic bird flying overhead. *Maybe he can help!* she thought. She waved her hand and tried to get the bird's attention.

The scout fairies looked to see what was going on. "Hawk! Hawk!" they yelled, sounding their warning horns.

Tink spotted a tree with a knothole and rushed straight for it.

When Vidia reached the end of
the tunnel, she could see the hawk
on a nearby branch. She stopped in
the nick of time—but Tink accidentally
slammed into her. Vidia went shooting out
of the tree. The hawk opened his beak, ready
to strike. Fairies pelted him with berries, rocks,
and twigs. Luckily, the bird flew away.

"Let me help you," Tink said to Vidia.

"I'm fine!" snapped Vidia.

"I was only trying to help," Tink explained.
She felt awful.

A little while later, Tinker Bell sat on the beach. "At this rate, I should get to the mainland right about, oh, *never!*"

Tink angrily threw a pebble into the bushes and heard a *CLUNK!* She went to investigate and found a beautiful porcelain box.

When her friends found
her, Tinker Bell was busy putting
all the gears and screws and springs back
inside the box. The final touch was attaching a
ballerina to the lid. Tinker Bell gave the dancer a spin,
and to her delight, the box played music!

"Do you even realize what you're doing?" asked Rosetta.
"Fixing stuff like this—that's what tinkering is!"

"Who cares about going to the mainland, anyway?"
Silvermist added.

But Tink still wanted to go.

Tink went to see the only fairy she thought might be able to help.

But Vidia was not in the mood for visitors—*especially* Tinker Bell.

"You're my last hope," pleaded Tink. "Rosetta won't even try to teach me to be a garden fairy."

That gave Vidia an evil idea. She suggested that Tinker Bell capture the Sprinting Thistles to prove that she would be a good garden fairy.

Tink knew that Vidia's plan was her last chance to go to the mainland. She set to work building a corral.

"Hi-yah! Git! Git!" Tinker Bell cried as she rode out into Needlepoint Meadow atop Cheese. She used two twigs to herd some Thistles into the corral. "It's working!" Tink cried joyfully. But as she headed back to the meadow, Vidia quietly blew open the corral gate. The Thistles ran away.

Soon other Thistles popped up to join the ones that had escaped. It was a stampede!

The Thistles headed toward Springtime Square, trampling over the carefully organized springtime supplies.

Everything was destroyed. And it was all Tinker Bell's fault.

"There isn't a garden fairy alive who can control those weeds!" Rosetta exclaimed.

"This has all gone too far," declared Silvermist.

Just then, Queen Clarion appeared. "By the Second Star! All the preparations for spring . . ."

"I'm sorry," Tinker Bell whispered as she took to the sky.

A little while later, Tink
went to the Pixie Dust Well.
She told Terence she was leaving
Pixie Hollow.

He kindly gave her a double scoop of the
glittering dust.

"Thanks, Terence," said Tink.

Terence was surprised she knew his name. "I'm just
a dust-keeper," he said, "not exactly seen as the most
important fairy in Pixie Hollow."

"You're probably the most important one there is!"
Tink argued. "Without you, no one would have any
magic! You should be proud!"

"I am," Terence replied.

Tink could tell that Terence knew she wasn't
proud of *her* talent.

Tink stopped in to visit the workshop one last time. She *did* love to tinker—even though her contraptions never worked.

Just then, she noticed that Cheese was sniffing something. It was the pile of trinkets she had found on the beach.

"Lost Things . . . that's it!" she cried. She went to her worktable and started to tinker.

That night, Queen Clarion gathered all the fairies.
She explained that spring would not arrive that year,
since there wasn't time to replace what had been ruined.
  "Wait!" Tinker Bell cried, landing in the middle of the
square. "I know how we can fix everything!"
  She demonstrated her paint sprayer, which she had
fixed so that it worked perfectly.

Tink had also designed speedy machines to fix the things the Thistles had trampled.

Vidia was furious. "Corral the Thistles . . . ," she muttered. "I should have told you to go after the hawk!"

Queen Clarion overheard this. She looked sharply at Vidia. "I think your fast-flying talent is well suited to chasing down each and every one of the Thistles," the queen said sternly.

Vidia flew away. All of a sudden, she had a lot of work to do.

The queen turned to Tinker Bell. "Are you sure you can do this?" she asked.

"I'm a tinker, and tinkers fix things," Tink replied confidently. "But I can't do it alone!"

Clank, Bobble, and all the fairies offered to help. Soon the square was filled with piles and piles of useful objects.

Tink showed a group of fairies how to assemble a machine to make berry paint.

As soon as all the pieces of the machine were put together, the berries were crushed, and dozens of buckets were filled to the brim with paint.

Next, Tink used a glove and a harmonica to make a vacuum. The fairies could use it to collect hundreds of seeds at a time.

Everywhere she looked, Tinker Bell could see baskets and buckets of springtime supplies. Her plan was working!

Early the next morning, Queen Clarion and
the ministers of the seasons flew to the square.
They couldn't believe their eyes—there were
more springtime supplies than they had ever seen!
As the sun began to rise, the Everblossom
opened, giving off a golden glow. It was time to take
spring to the mainland! The fairies cheered.
"You did it, Tinker Bell!" Queen Clarion exclaimed.
"We *all* did it," Tink replied.

"Can't Tink come with us?" Silvermist asked.

"It's okay," Tink protested. "My work is here."

Fairy Mary gave a little whistle, and Clank and Bobble appeared with the music box.

"Actually ran across this myself many seasons ago," said Fairy Mary. "Didn't have a clue how to fix it. But you did, Tinker Bell. And I'd imagine there's someone out there who's missing this. Perhaps a certain tinker fairy has a job to do after all . . . *on the mainland.*"

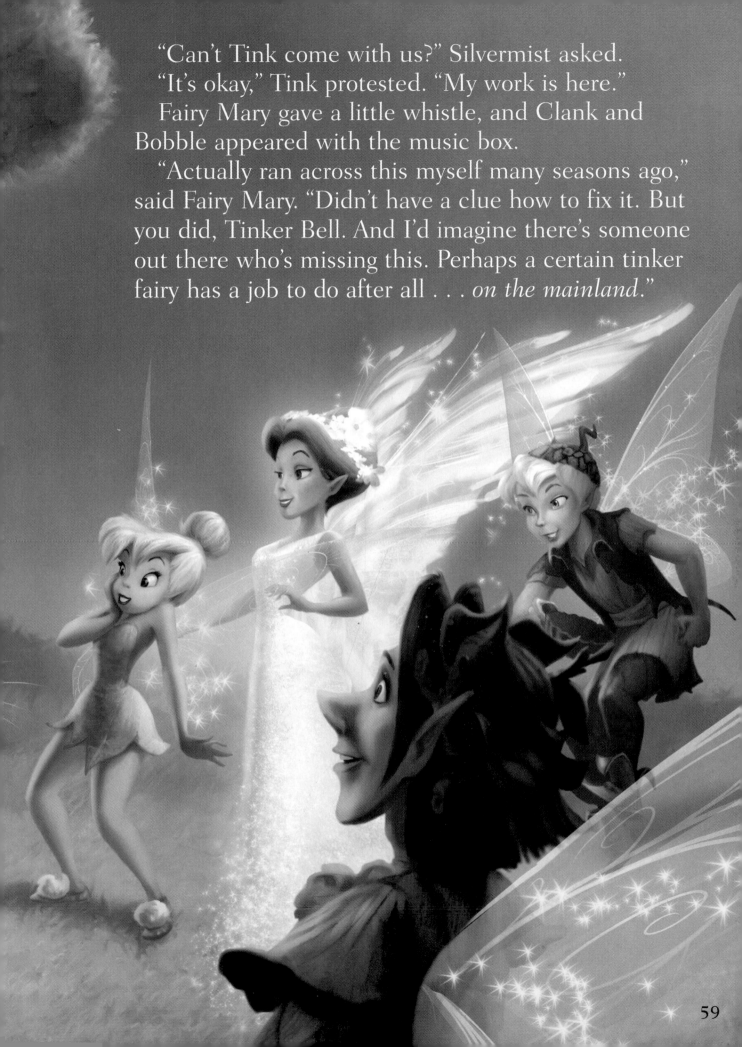

Tink and the other fairies flew toward London. When they arrived, everything was cold and the landscape was gray.

The fairies spread out across the city. A light fairy melted the frost on a tree branch. A water fairy sprinkled pixie dust on a frozen pond to thaw the ice. The animal fairies gently woke the hibernating creatures tucked inside the trees. Soon flowers bloomed and baby birds took flight. Tink was amazed by the magic her friends created.

Now it was time for Tinker Bell to make her special delivery. She sprinkled some of the extra pixie dust Terence had given her on the music box, to make it fly.

As Tink passed a bedroom window, both she and the music box began to glow. Tink knew that the owner of the music box must live there. She set the box on a windowsill and peered into the room.

Tink tapped on the glass and ducked out of sight. In a few moments, a little girl named Wendy Darling poked her head out the window.

Wendy's face filled with happiness. She took a small key from a chain around her neck and turned it in a slot. The music box began to play!

The fairies' work was done. It was time for them to return to Never Land.

From then on, Tink used her rare talent to make the lives of everyone in Pixie Hollow just a little bit better. She was proud to be a tinker fairy!